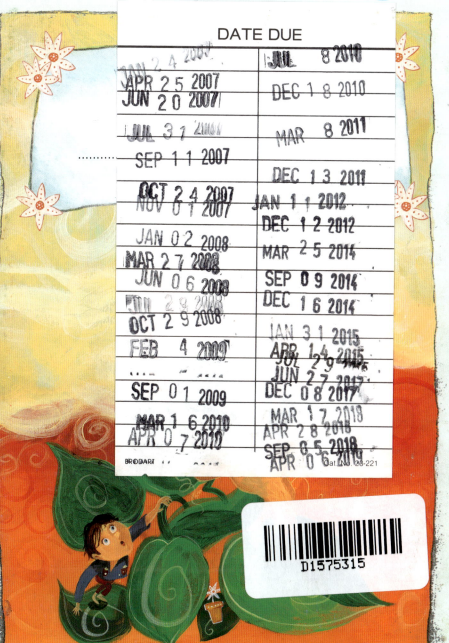

This is the story of Jack Pott.

You can read a little or read a lot!

There's something else.

Can you guess what?

Throughout this book there's

a flowerpot to spot.

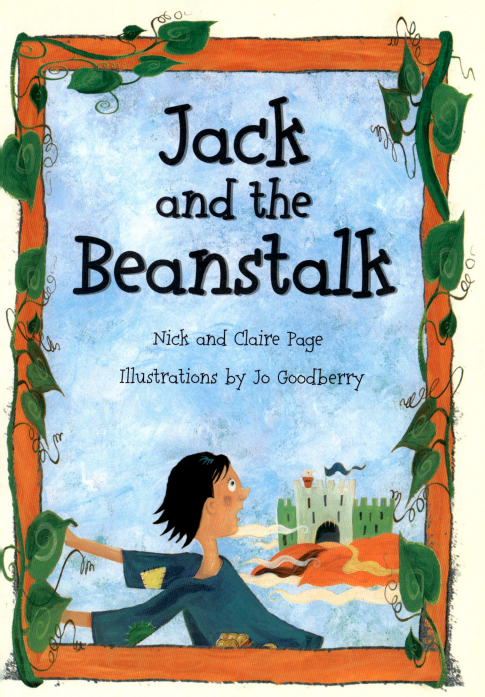

Jack
and the
Beanstalk

Nick and Claire Page

Illustrations by Jo Goodberry

make
believe
ideas

Jack Pott was very poor. He lived in a shed with his mother, Dotty, and a cow called Skimmed Milk.

But Skimmed Milk wasn't giving
any milk. So Dotty sent Jack to sell
Skimmed Milk at the market.
Jack met a little old lady who said,
"Give me that cow and
I'll give you these
magic beans."
"Magic," said Jack.

Mother Goose
Traditional

Fairy Tale
SEEDS

Magic
Beans

PACK of 5

"Mom!" said Jack. "Look what I got for Skimmed Milk!"
Dotty could not believe it.
She threw the beans out the window and sent Jack to bed without supper.

Next morning, it was dark outside.
Looking out, Jack saw why!
A big beanstalk had sprung up in the
garden and reached up to the sky.

Jack climbed the beanstalk
to see where it led. At the
top, floating on a cloud, was
a huge castle. In a massive
room inside the castle stood
a tall table and chair.

"Someone BIG lives here," said Jack. Then he saw a treasure chest full of gold! Jack grabbed the gold and put it in his pockets.

12

Suddenly the door burst open
and a gigantic giant marched in.
He had a horrible head, enormous
eyes, nasty nostrils, terrible teeth,
legs like lampposts, and a bulging
pot-belly. He was as tall as a tree
and as big as a bus!

The giant stood still. Then he roared:
"Fee fi fo fum,
I smell the blood of an Englishman.
Be he alive or be he dead,
I'll mix his bones into my bread."

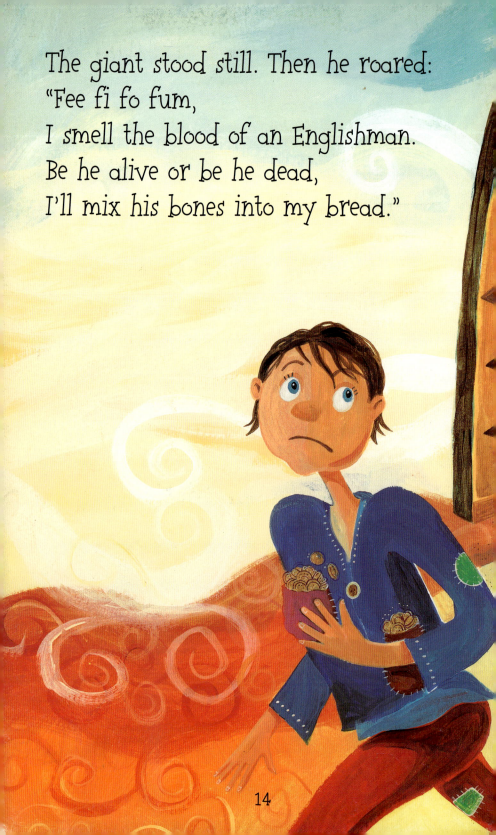

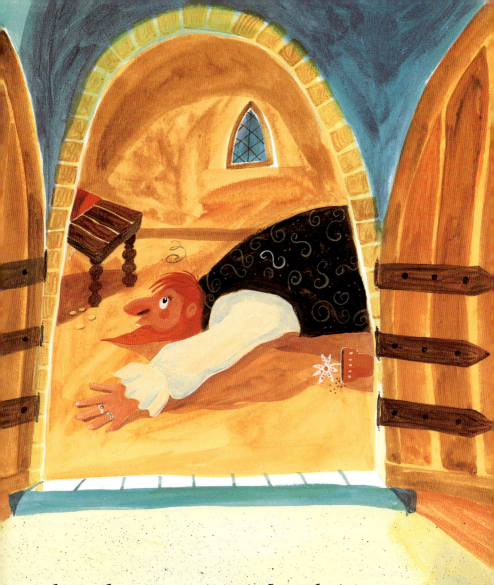

Then the giant spotted Jack in
the chest. Jack jumped out and ran.
The giant tripped and fell over
with a terrible crash!

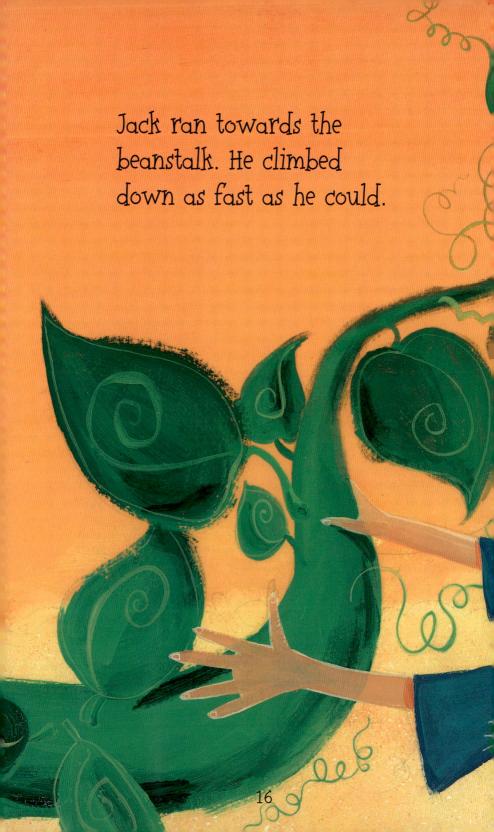

Jack ran towards the
beanstalk. He climbed
down as fast as he could.

But the giant began
to follow him. Jack
heard the giant roar:

"Fee fi fo fum,
I smell the blood of an Englishman.
I'll have him flattened, I'll have him fried,
I'll have boiled with a salad on the side!"

At the bottom of the beanstalk, Jack shouted to his mother: "Get an axe!"
"You mustn't play with axes!" said his mother. "It's dangerous!"
"No," said Jack. He pointed to the giant. "That's dangerous!"

Jack and his mother heard a roar:
"Fee fi fo fum,
I smell the blood of an English Mom!
I'll have her steamed,
I'll have her stewed,
I'll have her boiled or barbecued!"

Jack chopped at the beanstalk.
His mother cut it with the bread knife.

21

There was a creaking and a
cracking and the beanstalk
fell like a tree. The giant fell
to the ground, quite dead.

The gold fell out of Jack's pockets.
"Look! Pots of money!" shouted Jack.
"We've hit the jackpot, Jack Pott!"
grinned his mother.

Jack bought back Skimmed Milk
from the little old lady. And Jack's
mother bought a big balloon and
went on day trips. But where
she went she would not say.

Ready to tell

Oh no! Some of the pictures from this story have been mixed up! Can you retell the story and point to each picture in the correct order?

Picture dictionary

Encourage your child to read these harder words from the story and gradually develop their basic vocabulary.

axe

beanstalk

castle

flowerpot

giant

market

mother

point

window

Key words

Here are some key words used in context.
Help your child to use other words from
the border in simple sentences.

They lived **in** a potting shed.

The cow was sold **at** the market.

He climbed **up** the beanstalk.

"**Look!**" said Jack.

They had lots **of** money.

Gold

Decorate a Dotty pot!

You may not be able to grow a giant beanstalk, but why not decorate a flowerpot and grow a plant of your own?

You will need

a medium-sized terracotta flowerpot and pot holder
• powder or poster paints in different colors
• craft glue • plastic cups • paintbrush

What to do

1 Make sure your flowerpot is clean and dry.

2 You are going to decorate the pot with paint mixed with craft glue. For each color mix $1/3$ glue to $2/3$ paint in a plastic cup. Use this to give the pot a waterproof and shiny "varnish" effect.

3 Paint the pot and holder with a base coat of one color and leave to dry.

4 When dry, use different colors to paint patterns on top of the base coat. You might like to make it as dotty as one of Dotty's dresses. Or you could paint it black and white like Skimmed Milk the cow. Leave until dry.

5 Find out at your local garden center what will grow at this time of year. (Perhaps they will say "magic beans!") Follow their advice about how to plant the bulb or seeds they suggest.

6 Water the pot regularly and wait for the plant to grow...